WHAT I LEAVE BEHIND

WHAT I

LEAVE BEHIND

Alison McGhee

A Caitlyn Dlouhy Book

atheneum   New York London Toronto Sydney New Delhi

atheneum

An imprint of Simon & Schuster Children's Publishing Division
1230 Avenue of the Americas, New York, New York 10020

Text copyright © 2018 by Alison McGhee
Cover illustration copyright © 2018 by Dana Svobodová
Chinese calligraphy by Sherman Ng

For information about special discounts for bulk purchases, please contact Simon & Schuster Special Sales at 1-866-506-1949 or business@simonandschuster.com.
The Simon & Schuster Speakers Bureau can bring authors to your live event. For more information or to book an event, contact the Simon & Schuster Speakers Bureau at 1-866-248-3049 or visit our website at www.simonspeakers.com.
Also available in an Atheneum hardcover
Book design by Sonia Chaghatzbanian and Irene Metaxatos
The text for this book was set in Archer.
The calligraphy for this book was rendered in brush, India ink, and Photoshop.
Manufactured in the United States of America
First Atheneum paperback edition May 2019
10 9 8 7 6 5 4 3 2 1
The Library of Congress has cataloged the hardcover edition as follows:
Names: McGhee, Alison, 1960– author.
Title: What I leave behind / Alison McGhee.
Description: New York : Atheneum, 2018. | "A Caitlyn Dlouhy Book." | Summary: Since his father's suicide, Will, sixteen, has mainly walked, worked at Dollar Only, and tried to replicate his father's cornbread recipe, but the rape of his childhood friend shakes things up.
Identifiers: LCCN: 2017001373 | ISBN 9781481476560 (hc) | ISBN 9781481476577 (pbk) | ISBN 9781481476584 (eBook)
Subjects: | CYAC: Grief—Fiction. | Stores (Retail)—Fiction. | Fathers and sons—Fiction. | Rape—Fiction. | Suicide—Fiction. | Single-parent families—Fiction.
Classification: LCC PZ7.M4784675 Dol 2018 | DDC [Fic]—dc23
LC record available at the https://lccn.loc.gov/2017001373

To the sweet memories
of Garvin Wong and Jeanyee Wong,
who filled my life with blessings
beyond measure

You ever had real cornbread?

Like from a cast iron skillet stuck in the oven to preheat while you mix the batter? A hot, hot oven. So hot that before you open the door you have to put oven mitts on your hands.

And when you take the cast iron skillet out, you pour in a little melted butter and it hisses, the skillet's that hot, and then you pour in the batter and it starts to brown and puff around the edges even before you put the skillet back in.

That kind of cornbread, that's the kind I mean.

You got your various cornbreads, my dad used to say. *You got your nonsweet southern, your sweetish northern. And then you got your dad's cornbread.*

The way he said it was like he was speaking in boldface. You know?

Dad's cornbread.

He used to put it together from a recipe in his head. Maybe I'll try to make it tonight. I do that sometimes, try to re-create the recipe. Try to make it come out the way his did.

I keep the cast iron skillet in my closet. Eggs in the fridge. Butter. No milk, but that's okay. Water works.

Sometimes you got to walk the day out of you. You know? Walk it right out through the soles of your feet.

Dollar Only's closed now, my shift is over, it's Tuesday night, which means my mom's got the overnight shift and she's not going to notice if I'm not home.

The night and its sidewalks are right out that door.

Wring out the mop, empty the bucket, sign out. Say goodbye to Major Tom, waiting to lock up and exit out the back door to his car.

Major Tom, he's not a walker. Most people aren't. But I am.

Tonight the air itself is dark. That happens sometimes. It's not just the lack of sun, it's the presence of darkness.

If you're a walker, a real walker, your feet can figure out the right route. Sometimes the right route is one that goes past the places you love, like the cathedral, like the park off Whittier, like the Grand Central Market and its stalls.

Sometimes the right route is the route *not* past other places, places you maybe love but can't walk by right now.

Like Playa's house.

Like the blessings store.

Like the river bridge over Fourth Street.

Let your feet find the way. You'll know it when they do. Then let the day drain out of you. Let whatever comes into your head just float around in there.

What's in there tonight? Cornbread. Black cast iron cornbread like my dad used to make.

And that raggy little blanket Playa used to carry to school in her backpack, back in elementary school.

And the case in the back of the blessings store, a hundred blessings all numbered in Chinese.

To unbreak your broken heart.

To make a cloud of safety around you.

To light at night for peace.

How I got the job at Dollar Only was I saw the ad posted in the corner of the window.

So why here? said Major Tom. *Why Dollar Only?*

I need to start saving up. College.

And where did you see our ad?

Well, I walk past here pretty much every day. On the way to school.

Ah, school. Where do you go?

Mountain High.

Oh yes? There's a song called "Rocky Mountain High." You ever hear it?

Um, yeah. My mom likes that song.

Well, you tell your mom she's got good taste! Can you work nights and weekends?

This interview was in Major Tom's office, which is what he calls it even though it's a closet next to the employee bathroom that he shoved a desk and roller chair into.

There's a big corkboard on the wall that he pins motivational quotes on.

If you can dream it, you can do it.

With the new day comes new strength and new thoughts.

A life lived without purpose is no life at all.

If at first you don't succeed, try, try again.

It's like he intentionally searched for the lamest quotes in the history of the world. You know?

Walk one day out and another day in: home, school, work.

At first I used to call Major Tom by his name, Mr. Montalvo.

But he doesn't want me to. *Call me Tom, Will!*

Which at first I interpreted as him wanting to be called Tom Will, which is weird. But no. Will's *my* name and Tom's his name, the name he wants me to call him.

I'd been there a week at this point, and already I knew that Dollar Only is pretty much his life.

Some people, they're like that. They smile in a kind of helpless way.

So I did what I do with people like Major Tom: jump in and start giving them shit. Then they feel included. Like they're part of the world, like they have actual friends. Like someone *sees* them.

Why I started calling him Major Tom?

Because he likes music, and he's about my mom's age, so I figure he must know that Bowie song, that "Space Oddity" one she loves. About Major Tom.

Bowie was old but cool. So a nickname like Major Tom would make Mr. Montalvo feel cool.

Which it does. Because how could it not? I mean, Bowie.

Music is the refuge of the lonely, my dad used to say.

That, and *Carry on, my wayward son.*

And *Don't let the bastards get you down.*

And a bunch of other things. But those are the ones I think about the most. Music isn't only the refuge of the lonely, but still, I know what he meant. Like with Major Tom.

"Ground control to Major Tom," I say over the loudspeaker when I need Mr. Montalvo at the register.

"Commencing countdown! Engines on!" is what he usually says. Right back over the loudspeaker. And then he hurries right over.

Sometimes he sings part of the song, the line about the spaceship knowing which way to go, and another one about how much he loves his wife.

Mr. Montalvo doesn't have a spaceship and he doesn't have a wife. But he loves it when I call him Major Tom.

Things aren't easy for Major Tom. Social skills kinds of things, you know?

Some things aren't easy for me, either, but that's not one of them. I know how to give people shit, when to step forward, when to pull back. It's like a dance where you're born knowing the steps.

Not Major Tom, though.

Sometimes, when I'm closing, I see him sitting there in his closet-slash-office. Going over the schedule. Writing e-mails. And every time he thinks he hears someone coming, he swivels around, with that awkward-person smile.

Once—it's really late because some kid spilled an entire bottle of detergent in Aisle 9—I see him close his eyes, jab his finger on one of his motivational quotes, then open his eyes and read it out loud. And nod. Like his socially awkward life will change now.

And honestly, I can hardly stand it. That little nod. You know?

Remember that cornbread your dad used to make?

That's what Playa said to me at that party.

It's been a long time since Mountain Elementary. Years since we used to play at each other's houses, back before the girls and boys split into separate factions. But me and Playa, we'll always be friends. You can't forget the elementary years.

Will? Remember?

She'd stuck a Bugle on each fingertip like we used to do when we were kids. She waved them in my face, like, *Remember this too?* She was talking loud over the music. Shouting, almost.

Yeah, Playa. I remember.

Walk and walk and walk the day out. It's like a mantra.

Like Major Tom with his *If at first you don't suc-ceed*, and like my dad with his *Don't let the bastards get you down*, and like Dear Mrs. Lin, which is what my dad called the lady at the blessings store, with her *Help you?*

Okay, maybe not like her. Been a long time since I was in the blessings store. A looong time. Maybe Dear Mrs. Lin's not even there anymore.

I'm almost home. Maybe I'll get out the skillet. Make my offering to the cornbread ghosts.

The hundred blessings display is at the back of the blessings store. Each numbered with a Chinese number.

It's been a long time since I was in there, spying on Dear Mrs. Lin when she was arranging them. Weird shit. Weird to my dad and me, anyway. Like a ceramic hand or a bunch of dried-up herbs. Each with a specific purpose.

Blessing for the dead.

Blessing for the afraid.

Blessing for the lost.

Why those blessings just popped into my head, who knows. *The mind, she works in mysterious ways.* Or so our third-grade art teacher used to say.

Cornbread fail. Too much cornmeal, not enough flour. Not enough butter, too much baking powder.

Shit, I don't know. I'm not the one who had the recipe in his head. I wrap it up in wax paper and walk to Dollar Only next day by way of First so I can give it to Superman.

Today Superman's sitting against the brick wall of the alley between City of Angels Guitar and Payday Loans.

"You hungry, Superman?"

He nods, bows his head, and I set it into his outstretched palms.

"Carry on, my wayward son," I say, and I keep moving.

There's this kid who lives over on State. I see him outside sometimes, if I'm walking by before a night shift. Scrubby little backyard with a couple random hibiscus stuck in it.

Black hair, brown skin, brown eyes. Skinny. Little smiley dude, is how I think of him. He's like six, maybe seven.

He's out there today. Alone. I figure I'll check on him.

"Hey, little dude, what's up?"

"Mister, come here!"

I'm sixteen, right? First time anyone's ever called me "mister."

"I'm waiting for the butterflies," he says. "Five butterflies land on the garage wall every day at 5:20."

I figure the little dude's maybe a tiny bit off, you know? But whatever. He's waiting for me to walk over to the chain-link fence he's standing by. So over I go.

"Watch, mister," he says. "They'll come."

I wait with him. Why not? I don't have to be at Dollar Only until 5:30. And hell if five butterflies don't appear right when the little dude said they would. I check my phone: 5:20.

"Whoa! You weren't shittin me, little dude."

Kid doesn't blink an eye. He just nods. Stares at the butterflies and smiles.

"Nope," he says. "I wasn't."

How weird is that? Five butterflies every day, and the little dude waiting for them. Like a miniature butterfly scientist or something. How did he even figure it out?

So we get this shipment of plastic binoculars the next day.

"Where do you want these, Major Tom? Toys or Tools?"

"Your call, Dollar Will," he says, with this huge smile. So proud he came up with that nickname. I picture him in his office-slash-closet, thinking it up.

I smile and shake my head like I'm blown away by his creativity, to make him happy. Which it does.

On to Toys.

I open the box with my box cutter, which isn't allowed in Dollar Only but which I bring anyway because screw that. And guess what? The binoculars have butterflies painted on them.

"Little butterfly dude!" I say out loud. That's my new name for him.

I buy a pair, then and there, 15% employee discount, which brings the total to $.85, and I go to the break room to stash them in my locker.

Major Tom's in his closet-slash-office. He swivels around. That hopeful look on his face.

"'Little butterfly dude,'" he says. "Is that a line from a song?"

He must have overheard me. Now he's hoping he's guessed right.

"Not yet," I say. "Maybe you're the man to write it."

When Major Tom smiles for real, like now, you can see his snaggle tooth. A story makes itself up in my head, him as a little kid and his mom making him grilled cheese and teasing him about his snaggle tooth, but in a nice-mom kind of way.

Music is the refuge of the lonely, I can hear my dad say in my head.

Don't let the bastards get you down, I tell him. Also in my head.

After I close—"**Time to leave the capsule, Major**
Tom," "Hang tight, Dollar Will!"—I take the alley home,
which ordinarily I wouldn't do, because obviously, but
I walk hard and tall, no earbuds, hand in pocket on my
box cutter, down the middle of the alley between State
and First.

The chain-link fence around the little dude's house
doesn't have a gate, which is weird. But that's good,
because whenever I see him, he's out there alone. I
ease the binoculars down into the weeds around one
of the random hibiscus near the garage.

There you go, little dude.

二十三

"Mister! Look what I got!"

It's the next day. He's rigged up a scraggly strap—looks like wool unraveled from an old sweater—and the binoculars are dangling around his neck.

"Holy shit! Where'd you get them?"

He looks at me like I'm dumb, like the answer's obvious.

"From the butterflies. They brought them when I was asleep."

Then he puts them up to his eyes. They cover his whole face—he's a tiny kid, little butterfly dude is—and I have to keep walking. It's like that night I saw Major Tom nodding at his motivational quotes. You know?

It was like our fifth-grade field trip to the La Brea Tar Pits. School bus jouncing its way across the city, purple jacarandas all in bloom.

José the fat kid sitting by himself, staring out the window, eating Cheese Doodles.

Crunchcrunchcrunchswallow. Crunchcrunchcrunch-swallow.

Then he finished the bag and turned and saw everyone laughing at him.

The look on his face.

Playa looked at me from her seat. She knew how I felt. She felt the same way.

That kind of thing has to be walked out through the soles of your feet. But I didn't know that yet, back then.

二十五

When Playa pushed through the crowd to ask about my dad's cornbread, I wondered—did she still think about him? All the cornbread he made for us?

I didn't answer. I left.

After I left the party, is when it happened.

To Playa, who I've known since kindergarten. To Playa, whose parents so love the beach they used to make up songs about it. Playa this, playa that. Hell if they didn't name their only baby Playa.

Life's a beach and then you die, I said once to Playa, giving her shit. She laughed. She always laughed at my jokes.

二十言

There was one Playa and three guys. Do I need to say anything else? No. I don't.

Her friend Angie got drunk and left without her. Playa fell asleep on a pile of jackets, waiting for her. *Angie got drunk and left without her. Playa fell asleep.* People keep saying that, angry at Angie.

"I don't care if Angie got drunk. I don't care if Playa fell asleep."

My mom. Slit-eyed. Quiet-voiced, which is her when she's most pissed.

"You're telling me that's why they locked the door and raped her? Like that's the only logical outcome? That's the *explanation*?"

三十七

She looked me up and down. She does that some- times. Like she's suddenly realizing that I'm male, and can I be trusted or am I just another rapist?

I waved my hand in front of her face, like, *Hello, look at me, I'm Will, your nonrapist son.*

Her face softened.

"I'm sorry, Will. It just enrages me. Were you at that party?"

"Yeah." The party was on a Tuesday mom-at-work night, a cornbread-attempt night. "But I left way early."

"Do you know them? These rapists?"

No. I don't know them. Not really.

Playa's the one I know. Or used to.

Today she brings it up again, saying how broken-hearted Playa's parents are, and have I talked to Playa.

About what? The rape? No. My dad? No. Corn-bread? No.

I haven't talked to Playa about anything real in years, but I don't tell my mom that. I pick up my box cutter and head to the door.

It's not like I don't think about it all the time. I can't always talk about things, though.

"Will? I'm sorry."

I stop at the door. Turn around.

"For what?"

But she's shaking her head. Like she doesn't even know what she's sorry for.

二十九

I go by way of State so I can see the little butter-fly dude, but he's not out today.

You know how sometimes someone's face comes into your head?

And it's like you can almost see them and almost hear their voice?

And you wish you *could* see them right at that moment? Like somehow the world would be instantly better?

That's how I feel about the kid, even though I don't know his name. Or if he's got parents or a pet lizard or whatever. Friends. Someone to play with, the way Playa and I used to play together.

Paolo and Sam and Kendrick.

Playa.

That's what they were known as last month. By names and nicknames: Pow. Sammy-boy. Kendrick, who's nickname-resistant. And Playa, who never had one to begin with.

Except not anymore.

Now Kendrick is the rapist. Pow and Sammy-boy, too. Playa's the victim. Her parents went with her to the police station.

"I'm glad they're pressing charges," my mom says, nodding. "But she's going to need to be tough."

Now I'm standing by the little butterfly dude's house, hoping he'll emerge, but the back door to his house—which is pale green and orange—stays shut.

The whole way to Dollar Only, I look up.

Make a point of looking up sometimes, artists, our third-grade art teacher, Miss Trebulon, used to say. She always called us artists. *It's a big world. Bigger than you think, and full of mystery.*

So up I look. The jacarandas are in bloom, and they're purple. The sky is blue. The palm leaves are green. The air smells like lemons. A helicopter's making that *thwap-thwap* sound, bending this way and that like a giant nosy insect.

High in the sky a sharp white contrail changes into a blur of soft marshmallows.

三十三

I push open the door and suck in a lungful of Dollar Only air with my eyes closed to see if I can predict what shipment arrived today. Bleach? Flavored lip gloss? Grape Kool-Aid? Room deodorizer? Sometimes my best guess is stale air, but not today.

Orange.

Sharp and clear and clean. Like a weed whacker that slices names in half, so that Pow is ow and Sammy-boy is ammy-oy and Kendrick turns into drick. Lowercase. Cut off at the knees.

Orange dish soap? That's my best guess. A case of it, with one leaking bottle.

I open my eyes.

三十三

Major Tom is standing like two feet in front of me, waiting for me to open my eyes.

"Clementine?" he says.

He holds his hand out to me. In the exact center of his palm is a peeled clementine. Not just peeled, but peeled in one continuous peel which has then been folded up around the sections of orange.

"You peel that, Major Tom?" I say, because you can tell how much he wants someone to admire it. "That's rad."

Rad because he'll love being called rad.

"I did!" he says, and he rocks forward on his toes with pride.

三十四

"You been holding out on us, Major Tom," I say, and I pop a section into my mouth.

He wants more, but I got no more for him. Not today. Today's a day when the jacaranda flowers and the marshmallow contrail and this smell of orange are going to have to get me through. I got nothing left.

He clears his throat. "Uh, Will?"

No, man. Read my mind.

"What's that I hear?" I say. "Is that Aisle 12, calling my name?"

I squint like I'm listening. "Why yes, that's my name," I say, "floating in a most peculiar way."

三十五

Major Tom smiles, because he always smiles when I use a line from the Bowie song, but it's not his usual smile.

"Listen, Will," he says, and it's clear that Aisle 12 is not going to get me before whatever Major Tom has to say gets said, "I heard about what happened."

I look at him.

"At that party," he says.

Uh-huh.

"I just," he says. "Well, I know the girl goes to your high school, and"—*and what*, is what I'm thinking, dreading one of his lame-ass quotes.

He surprises me, though.

"And I'm sorry" is all he says.

三十三

Unloading shipment is where the forbidden box cutter comes in. One *zip* down the tape and *poof,* open.

Like the boxes have been waiting to see the world, and here's their chance.

I don't look at the outside labels before I open them. That way, the contents are a surprise.

"What might you hold, mystery box?" I say, talking to this one to keep things interesting. *Zip.* The flaps spring open.

Cornmeal.

Jesus. Really?

Look around, artists, Miss Trebulon used to say. *The world is full of mystery.*

Planet Earth is blue, Bowie says, *and there's nothing I can do.*

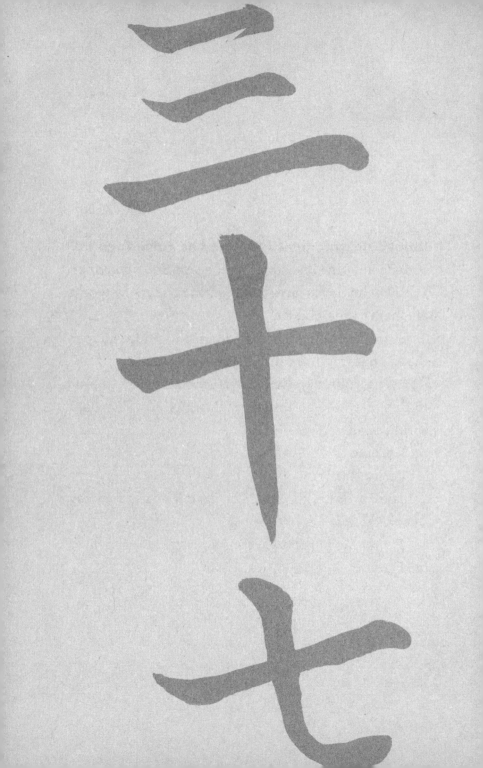

"Will? Cornmeal belongs in Aisle 3, doesn't it?"

"It does, Major Tom, it does indeed."

Major Tom is correct. Cornmeal does not belong here in Aisle 7, Household Goods, but how is a Dollar Only employee supposed to know that until he opens up that mystery box and knows what he's dealing with, right?

Major Tom looks at me with a tiny question in his eyes. I smile so he knows I'm not making fun of him.

Because I'm not. I'm thinking about the blessings store and whether this box full of cornmeal is like a blessing for the dead.

三十八

Some days are just-get-through-them days. You focus only on what's right in front of you, like sealed boxes and the box cutter *zipping* down each seal.

But cornmeal? Seriously?

Every time I've tried to make my dad's cornbread, it comes out bad. Too dry, too gummy, too salty or not salty enough. Tastes like shit, to be honest.

But I'm thinking about the black cast iron frying pan, and a box of cornmeal is in my hand. Major Tom's corkboard appears in my mind. *If at first you don't succeed, try, try again.*

Jesus. That is a truly terrible saying.

三十九

"Mommy? Why's that man talking to himself?"

"Some people like to talk to themselves, honey. Mommy does that herself sometimes!"

False cheer. That bright, don't-scare-the-kid tone. She looks at me with a fake smile. Nervous eyes.

I smile back, a real smile, and I shake my head, shrug, like *Hey, I know how you feel. I'd be weirded out too if I came across a Dollar Only employee standing there talking to a box of cornmeal.*

"Sorry, ma'am."

I don't even try to explain. Because what is there to say? Some people *do* talk out loud to themselves. Like Superman.

"Mommy? Why does the man have a knife?"

Oh, jeez. The box cutter.

"It's not really a knife," I say. "It's a box cutter. I use it to open boxes."

"See how careful he is?" says the mom. "Careful with the sharp edge?"

She's holding the kid's hand at this point. I'm trying hard not to look like a disturbed youth, because I'm not a disturbed youth. A distracted youth, maybe. A sad youth, maybe. An angry youth, sometimes. But disturbed? No.

"Your mom's right," I say. "Always be careful with sharp things."

Backup for the mom. Moms like that.

I flick the blade open and snick it down the tape, but this time I don't let the box spring open.

"You want to do the honors?" I say to the little kid, and she nods. Okay then. She reaches out and folds back the flaps.

"Well, well, what have we here?" I say.

Jump ropes. Dozens and dozens. Striped, each with a different-colored plastic handle: blue, yellow, pink, green. Little-kid colors.

The kid wants one. You can see it in her eyes. I hold out the box.

"If you could pick any jump rope, which one would you pick?"

Kid points at a purple-handled one.

"Be right back," I say to the mom. "Commencing countdown, engines on."

"Hey! I love that song!" she says, and now she's totally on my side.

Up to the register, out with the dollar, ring it up, bring it back.

"Now it's time to leave the capsule if you dare," I say, and I hand over the paid-for jump rope.

The mom's smiling, the kid's jumping rope right there in Aisle 7, and just then the little butterfly dude flashes into my head. The way he sits there, hands folded, waiting for the butterflies.

四十三

Playa and me, we're both sixteen. Her birthday is one day after mine in September.

How I know this is because we were the youngest kids in our kindergarten class. The cutoff was September 1 and we were born one week after, but our parents talked to the principal and got exceptions for both of us.

Supposedly because we could both print all the letters, upper- and lowercase, and we knew our colors and shapes.

But really because they didn't want to pay for day care anymore. Who can blame them, right? Shit's expensive, as my dad used to say.

Our dads, they were buddies after that, in a Fight the Power kind of way. Two brave men who took on the Man at Mountain Elementary and won.

At kindergarten Moving Up Day, Playa wore a yellow dress and black, shiny shoes. She had a white bow in her hair. Gold earrings. How I know this is because she stood on the back riser right next to me. We were both in the tall kids section.

I kept on being tall, but by the time we were in fifth grade, Playa was one of the short girls.

She's still short.

四十五

You know what's weird? That something—something *big*—can happen to someone you know, someone you've known forever, while you're just living your ordinary life, and you don't even know it's happening.

Like the party. I was *at* that party. I *left* that party. I was in the *same room* as Playa. We were breathing the same air. She was talking about my dad's cornbread.

Then I left and Playa stayed and ow and ammy-oy and drick walked in. And they raped her.

And shouldn't I have felt something? Some kind of shiver in the universe? Shouldn't I have known?

四十宗

I felt that way about my dad, the day it happened.

The day what happened, Will?

Shut up. *Say it. Just say it.*

The day he died, okay? That day. Like, wait, what? I mean, I just *saw* him. That morning. He was sitting at the table, drinking coffee and eating leftover corn-bread on a green plate.

"You want some cornbread, son? I'm famous for it, you know."

"Nah."

That plate isn't around anymore.

I don't know what happened to it.

Except that I do. I threw it away. I couldn't stand to look at it anymore, after that day.

四十七

Every time I used to open up the cabinet and see it sitting there, I saw my father sitting there, at the table. Drinking his coffee. Eating leftover cornbread.

Nah.

That was the last thing I said to my dad. I refused his cornbread. Don't tell me it's not important, don't tell me that's a stupid thing to care about, don't tell me my dad would understand, don't tell me to give up on the fucking recipe. You are not the one who stood there late to school on the last day you would see your dad and said *NAH.*

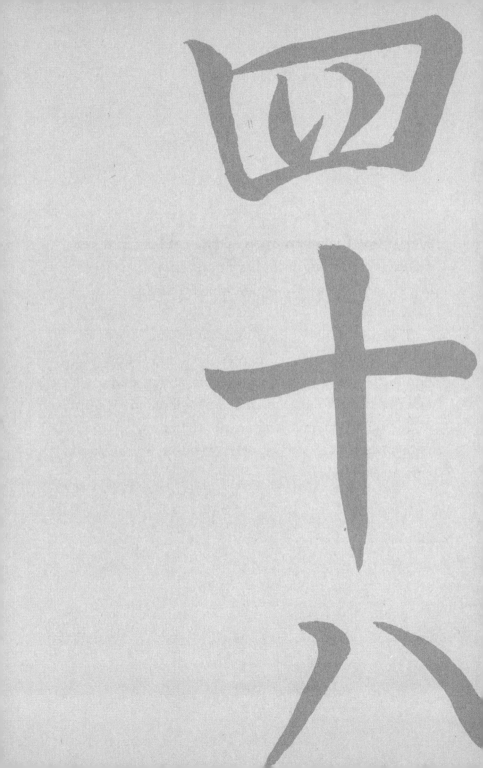

After the jump-rope kid's gone, I get an idea. It goes like this:

What if every single day, Playa gets a gift? One day a jump rope, another day a bar of soap that smells like lemons, the next day a pack of stickers. I could leave them on her doorstep after my shift. A hundred gifts for Playa.

I mean, picture her waking up. Still sleepy and maybe there's kitchen noise—her room is down the hall from the kitchen, I know this from back in the day—and everything's normal, everything's okay.

And then she remembers what happened.

四十九

At some point she has to walk out of the house into invisible air, air that has no roof or walls.

And how do you get through? You know? When things are too much?

Because the world, it's full of air. Full of sky and space. Ocean, too. All of which are bigger than any crowd of human beings, on the street, at school, at Dollar Only, at restaurants. At parties.

It's hard to remember that, though. Hard to remember that people are tiny. They stare at you, they talk about you, but all they are? Tiny.

Look up, artists.

In kindergarten Playa loved yellow. Yellow clothes, yellow notebooks, yellow barrettes. Maybe she quit yellow after elementary school, but screw it, I pick out a yellow jump rope for her.

The entire shift I'm unloading shipment, aisle to aisle, and in each aisle something else says *Playa* to me.

A three-pack of stickers.

A bag of caramels.

Some socks with flowers and hearts and green frogs on them. Kid socks. But Playa's small; maybe they'll fit.

At the end of my shift I bring the basket up to the cash register. Then I think, *tissue paper. And little gift bags.*

Gift bags, ten for $1.

A mere $10 for a hundred. What the hell, why not?

Tissue paper: pink, purple, yellow, white. Those are the colors of the tissue paper assortment in Aisle 13: Party Supplies.

Most hotels don't have a thirteenth floor, did you know that? Superstition. Bad luck.

But here's the thing: of course they do. Like there's a gap in the sky where the thirteenth floor should be? Thin air? No, man. What they do is label it the fourteenth floor.

So next time you're on the fourteenth floor of a building, just know that you're not.

五十三

After my shift, I keep going for a little while
after clocking out. The floors by Aisle 8: Pet Supplies
are dusty from a litter spill. I mop them. Mop. Mop.

"Dollar Will. Time for you to go home, isn't it, son?"

Oh fuck.

He's trying out *son* on me. You can hear it in his
voice, like he's been thinking about it for a while.

The sound of the word coming out of him makes
me think of a million things—does Major Tom want a
kid? Does he imagine himself as a dad? Calling some
little kid *son*?

五十三

And if Major Tom does want a kid, what about all the other things that have to come first? Like a girl. A girl who'd look at him and want to be with him.

Oh fuck. No.

"Ground control to Major Tom," I say. "These floors needed a shine. It's a dirty job, but someone's gotta do it."

Major Tom loves shit like that. Talk about yourself in the third person, hold an imaginary mic to your mouth. He smiles right away, just like I knew he would.

I smile back. But not really. Not tonight. Tonight, it's too much.

五十四

He surprises me, though. He stands there watch- ing me swab for a while—swabbie's a sailor word, isn't it?—and then he reaches out and takes the mop from me.

"Go home, Dollar," he says.

Surprising. A tone in his voice I haven't heard before. There's nothing tentative in him at that moment, which is so unlike the way I think of Major Tom that I do it, I just let him take the mop.

"Okay," I say.

Then, weirdness, I tell him that I'm going to go home and make some cornbread. He nods, like, sure, that's entirely normal.

五十五

One more thing before I go. A red plastic step-stool and a blue shovel for the little dude. Can't forget about the little dude.

Out I go with my backpack stuffed. If everything's a dollar, that means everything's special or nothing's special. Right?

Back home there's a note on the table.

Love you, Willy. Xoxoxo, Mom.

The pen's still on the notepad, so I write her back.

Love you too, Mama.

Okay, cornbread, show me what you got. This time I add green chiles and sriracha. The butter hisses when it hits the hot pan, but the cornbread? Still sucks.

The last time I saw my dad, the day of the coffee mug and the green plate and him saying, *You want some cornbread, son?* and me saying *Nah*, he was doing the Jumble, same as every morning.

It was the day before's Jumble, because we don't get the newspaper, but Eddie next door does, and Eddie's one of those people who folds it up after he reads it so it looks exactly the same as when it's first unrolled. And then he carries it out to recycling and opens the lid and lowers it in.

Like a newspaper coffin.

Every night before bed, my dad used to go out and raise up Eddie's newspaper from the recycling dead.

He never read the news. Just the comics. Then, the next morning, he would do the Jumble. In pen. Which he was proud of, even though between you and me? The Jumble is not hard. At all.

"Why don't you read the news?" I asked him once.

"Don't bother with the goddamn news, son," he said. "We soak that shit in through our skin. Can't avoid the goddamn news if you want to."

My dad was a big fan of swearing.

五十六

It bugs the shit out of me when anyone tries to call me *son*. Major Tom was testing it out. He'd worked up his courage to say it. You can tell he wants to be someone's dad.

But the thing is, he can't be *my* dad. I already had a dad, and there's not ever going to be another one.

I didn't say anything, though. I mean, it's Major Tom, right? Major Tom who sat in his closet-slash-office that night closed-eyed and pointed to one of his shitty quotes and then nodded. You know?

The guy kills me, almost literally.

五十九

How do you get through, when things are too much? Ask me and I'll tell you to walk.

"Just walk," I'll say. "Walk. Walk and walk and walk and walk and walk."

That's what I did, after my dad. The morning after they found him, the morning after the night that my mom stayed up all night and I tried to stay up with her but I fell asleep against my will, was the morning of the day that I started walking.

I was thirteen years old when I began to walk. And now I'm sixteen and I'm still walking.

Another note:

Smells good in here. You been baking?
Love, Mom.

Jesus, Mom. Am I sitting in a tin can? Far above the world?

No. I have not been baking cornbread on Tuesdays when you're working the overnight, because only one person knew the recipe for that cornbread, and it cannot be replicated. The cast iron skillet is not buried in my closet under the Bowie T-shirt that I don't wear anymore, and the Dollar Only cornmeal is not shoved in my sock drawer.

Everything above is a lie except the can't be replicated part.

Carry on, my wayward son.

Next night after my shift, I'm walking in the direction of Playa's house—because the gift giving starts tonight, right?—when the dog of insanity begins his insane barking. I'm still two blocks away, but wow. The block he lives on is loud to begin with, but still.

The dog of insanity lives on a big chain that runs from the orange tree in the backyard of his shitty house to the chain link fence in front.

Zip.

Back and forth, back and forth he races, the metal clip on his metal collar zipping along the chain.

Zip. Zip. Zip.

I'd be a man of insanity if I was chained up all day.
How would I ever walk my way out of things? Answer:
I wouldn't.

You know what, dog-of-insanity owners? Fuck you.

You know what else? That dog needs a gift.
Deserves a gift. All alone in the dark like that, zipping
back and forth on the dirt track he's worn into the yard.
I decide to give him one of Playa's. Why not, right?
She's got no idea.

Besides, Playa wouldn't mind. Because she's Playa.

Hence, this orange spiky rubber ball. This one's for
you, dog of insanity.

言
十
三

Back when I started walking, my mom didn't
mention it. I figured she was so distracted that she literally didn't notice when I started disappearing for hours.

But now I think she knew. Because that's when the notes started.

Love you, Willy.
Sleep tight, Willy.
Mama loves Will.
Et cetera.

It's different, suicide. It's a different kind of death. Most people, they'll do anything to stay alive, right? Past the point where you're looking at them and thinking, *Wow. Your life must* suck. *Don't you, like, want to die?*

But most people don't. They just want to keep on living.

Except not everyone.

My dad had a note in the back pocket of his pants. His khakis, which he never wore because, like, my dad? Khakis? No. But there you have it. There was a lot of that back then. Confusion. Weirdness. I guess there still is.

If you had known my dad, which obviously you didn't, you would have laughed at the idea of him wearing khakis. Just not him.

But what *was* him? You know? Someone kills himself, someone who just seemed, I don't know, happy?— you look back and you start to question things. Like old photos.

Like at my seventh birthday party, the party Playa's dad was at too.

That one photo where my dad's wearing the mullet wig and laughing. Really laughing. Like giantly laughing, and his hand's on my shoulder.

Was he happy?

That's the kind of thing that comes into your mind when someone kills himself. Like, was it all pretend? Or was he happy for real, and did something just change one day and boom, **done**.

The note said:

I'm so sorry. I'm so so so so sorry.

So it was a for-real suicide. That note proves it. Otherwise we wouldn't know.

We would have wondered forever. Like did somebody jump him, some psychopath who decided to shove the guy in the dumb khakis up against the Fourth Street Bridge over the ditch known as the Los Angeles River and then heave him right over it?

At least I would've wondered.

Because without that note, I honestly don't think I would've believed my dad killed himself. I would have thought there was some psychopath out there, walking around, remembering the day he killed my dad. So in a way I guess I'm glad he wrote the note.

In a way.

You know?

One block from here, past the dog of insanity's house, past the park, past Playa's, is where when I was thirteen I started walking.

Down our block, cross the street, down the next block and the next and the next I went, like I was going to the park like always, but then I just kept on going.

Every step at that point was new.

The whole world was new and where it was new began eight blocks from my house, because me and my dad had never walked there together.

I was on my own. Like it or not.

Walking, walking, and walking, me and my shorts and my flip-flops and the Bowie T-shirt, which I wore literally every day back then. I stole it out of my dad's drawer after he died.

In the world beyond the one where my dad and I used to walk together, I didn't have to think about how sad my mom was, didn't have to think how my last word to him was *Nah*, and shit, that whole not-thinking thing? A huge relief.

Carry on, my wayward son.

Music is the refuge of the lonely.

You want some of my famous cornbread?

六十九

A whole bunch of little presents are coming for you, Playa. One per night. An anonymous friend hopes you like them.

Taco Loco. Estela's Panaderia. Libros Schmibros. PAWN PAWN PAWN Bring Us Your Gold and Your Silver! McDonald's.

Keep walking, feet. You know the way to Playa's house. Well, here we are. Hello, front steps. Here's a little white gift bag for Playa. Gift #1. Cookies. Cream-filled chocolate and vanilla, a sleeve of each wrapped up in cellophane with a picture of a smiling Asian baby girl. Yellow tissue paper.

And a note.

Don't let the bastards get you down.

On the way home I backtrack past them all: McDonald's now with Wi-Fi, PAWN PAWN PAWN, Libros Schmibros, Estela's Panaderia, Taco Loco.

Past the sketchy hotel, past the other hotel, past the construction site. Then I decide to detour up the hill. It's late, but screw it. Walk. Walk on. Walk tall.

Because little butterfly dude.

I miss him. You know?

Down the alley off State, even though no way would he be out at this time of night. Right up to his fence I go, though, and the security light clicks on and I look in, and ... holy shit.

Damn. Little dude's set himself up an altar.

The new red stepstool is set next to a baby agave that he must've just planted with the new blue shovel. Dirt still on it.

Can't you see it, the little dude out there, digging away with his plastic shovel?

Stepstool. Shovel. Little dude probably thinks they dropped down from heaven. And then I see the butterfly binoculars, set in the middle of the stepstool. Ready for the visitation.

I stand so long the security light blinks off. There's a faint light glowing upstairs in the little dude's house. A night-light, maybe.

Then, holy shit, kid's standing in the window, silhouetted against the light. He can't see me, right? I stop myself from calling, "Little dude!"

It's late. It's dark. Kids need sleep.

It's just when I'm mentally telling him to go back to bed that he waves. This little tiny wave, like *Hey, mister. I know it's you.*

Sometimes do you wish there was like an early warning system? So when certain things are coming up, you'd know? And then you could close your eyes and keep them closed until you're past the thing that's going to claw at your heart?

七十三

Playa. The little dude. Might as well check on the dog of insanity as long as we're on the topic. Right?

Oh my freaking God does he love that toy.

Zip.

That's the dog of insanity racing along his chain to me at the back fence. That orange blur? The spiky ball clenched in his jaws.

Back and forth he goes. Sometimes he drops the ball, you can tell it's deliberate, then pushes it with his paw. Like he's trying to convince himself that it's alive. Which must work, because then he dives on it again and off he goes.

Early warning system, please.

Because Major Tom and his motivational quotes, and the little dude and his altar to the butterfly gods, and my dad's green plate, and the dog of insanity loving his toy so goddamn much, that kind of thing?

Gets in my brain and never goes away.

Ground control to Major Tom

Your circuit's dead, there's something wrong

Playa's in my brain, and she will never go away either.

This goes way back, to when we were little. And it has nothing to do with what happened at the party. This is before that. Second grade. Recess.

七十五

Most people can't do the rings.

There're a few exceptions. Like the little lightweight kids who grab the first ring, then propel themselves forward, one hand grabbing the next ring, then the next—*swing—swing—swing*—one ring after another until

Drop

—and they're back in the sand looking around, like *Did I just do that?* And the answer is, Yes, you did. You just triumphed.

But like I said, most people can't do the rings. Most people—adults and kids alike—you heave them up, and then they just . . . hang there.

Playa could do them, though. That girl? Badass.

She leaped right up—no help, no hesitation—and she clenched both hands around the first ring while she kicked her legs back and then

    Ring

    Ring

    Ring

One after the other after the other, and she dropped down to the sand: **Done.** She brushed her hands off and then—I saw this because I was watching her from the top of the fort next to the rings—she clapped for herself. This tiny little clap, just the tips of her fingers clapping against each other. You could see her lips moving, whispering, *Yay, Playa!*

Early warning system, please. Please.

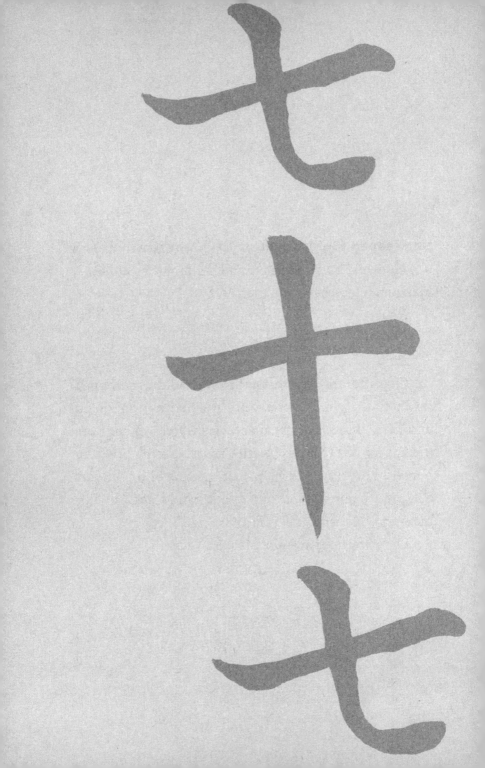

No one saw her do it. A Kick the Can game was taking up most of the playground, and there were just a few of us not playing. She probably thought she was alone.

Then *boom*, she looked up and she saw me watching her. I knew the exact look in her eyes: happiness to fear to suspicion to shutdown in half a second.

The kind of look where you have to do something instantly or you know she's never going to look at you again, she's going to avoid you forever. You know?

And so I did something instantly.

せ

キ

ハ

What I did was I nodded. I was up in the fort and I just looked her right in the eye, and I nodded. That's all you need to do, I guess.

It's simple.

But not. Because it sets something in motion and then it lasts forever. Like with me and Playa. That yellow dress on kindergarten Moving Up Day. The rings in second grade.

Like my dad's green plate and those khakis and the risen-from-the-dead Jumble and that fucking cornbread that I can't make for shit.

All of it. That stuff just burns and burns its way into you.

七十九

So ow confessed. Then ammy-oy. Then drick. Sentencing to come.

Playa's back in school. Her friends walk her every-where.

Bird-of-paradise notecards. Hairbands. Bendy straws. These are the things I leave for her. And the same note every night: *Don't let the bastards get you down.*

Major Tom tilts his head out of his closet-slash-office.

"You okay, Dollar?"

He didn't call me *son.* I'll give him that.

"We good, Major Tom, we good."

Confuse him with the *we* thing, shall we? Speak like Yoda in our heads, shall we? Put our hands together and bow in a namaste-like manner, shall we?

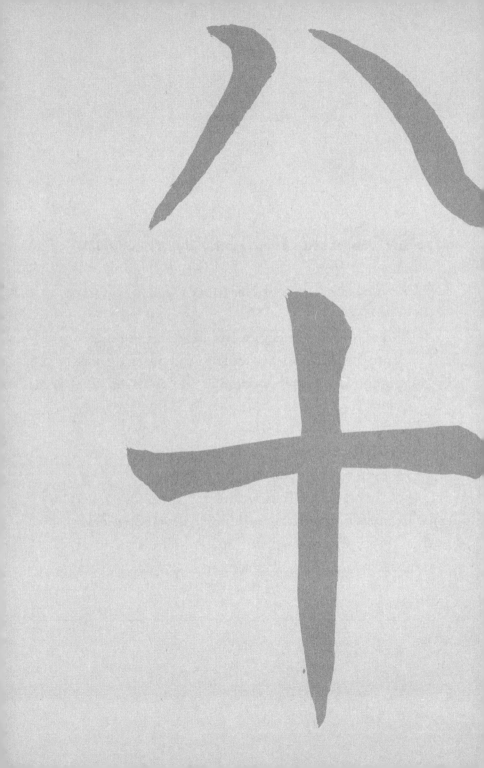

And what does Major Tom do?

Fist-bumps me. Big smile on his face. You can just tell how long he's wanted to fist-bump someone. And now his chance has come.

Oh, Major Tom. You're gonna kill me. Swear to God.

If he hadn't done that—tried once again to be a cool, unlike-himself guy—I probably would've walked straight home after leaving Playa's gift on the steps instead of where I do go, which is straight past Grand Central Market, Eggslut, and all the other food stalls and straight into Taco Loco, where I buy myself two tacos. Taco Tuesday.

And then I detour into the blessings store, which is what we called it when we were little and which is what I still call it. Old habits.

"Help you?"

That's Dear Mrs. Lin. She doesn't recognize me. How would she? It's been a long time.

"Nah. Thank you."

She nods and goes back to what she's doing, which involves a pile of narrow red strips of paper and a gold stamper thing. Lots of red in Asian stores.

Is the hundred blessings case still in the way back? Maybe they got rid of it.

But no. It's still here.

八十三

A couple of girls and their boyfriends are examining the hundred blessings, reading them aloud, studying the weird little bottles and candles.

I wait until they finish staring and pointing and laughing. Until the string of bells on the door jingles, which means they've left the store. Until there's only the *stamp stamp stamp* of Dear Mrs. Lin's gold stamper. She's industrious as hell, Dear Mrs. Lin. Never stops working.

Now it's my turn. Hello, blessings. And so we meet again.

To unbreak your broken heart.

To make a cloud of safety around you.

To light at night for peace.

八十三

"Help you?" Dear Mrs. Lin says again when I get to the counter, still not looking up from her red paper, her gold stamper.

"Yeah. These."

She picks up each one, turns it around, examines it, rings each one up separately on the old cash register, even though all the blessings cost a dollar.

Ding.

Ding.

Ding.

She wraps each one up in white tissue paper and puts them in a plastic bag with the blessings store logo on it, which is the glowing-eyed face of some creepy-looking saint or angel or devil. Human, maybe? Sometimes you can't really tell.

"You're a good friend," Dear Mrs. Lin says.

"Excuse me?"

She touches the bag with her finger that's all gold from the stamp pad.

"These are for a friend, yes?"

"Maybe. Yeah."

"See? I know."

Then she looks up at me, and honest to God, she breaks into this huge grin. Like, I didn't even know Dear Mrs. Lin knew how to smile. It's like smiling's a learned skill and she never mastered it. Like a check-box on an elementary school report card that was always unchecked when it came to her.

But she's looking right at me and smiling.

八十五

"You were little when I first see you. All this time you come in for blessings. So many years!"

She hands the bag to me.

"Good friend, good friend. I know."

I'm almost out the door when she calls to me.

"Your father? Why I don't see him anymore?"

She's holding her gold-stained palm off the floor at the invisible line that's me when I was a little kid. Because it was my dad I used to come here with.

I shrug. Shake my head. Hold the bag of blessings tight to my chest and out the door I go.

Back in second grade, it took Playa a second, maybe three, but then she smiled back at me. Her front teeth were missing—we all had a few teeth gone, it was the tooth fairy stage of life—and that smile was gigantic.

I could see why she didn't smile much. Because when she did? It took over her whole face. Her whole body. She turned from a girl into a smile.

That was a long, long time ago. We were seven years old. But Playa, she knew right then, and she knew I knew, that I had her back.

八十七

Here's what I think about sometimes: If I'd said *Sure* instead of *Nah*, would my dad still have jumped?

It's an answerless question, like lots of questions. Why did he jump? Did he feel like no one had his back? Even though he had my mom and me and a thousand other friends—because my dad, he was one of those charming people who everyone loved—did he feel alone?

Did he feel like he was one thing on the outside and something else entirely different on the inside?

Does Major Tom feel that way?

Does Playa?

Do I?

Sometimes.

But what if it's more than sometimes? Like what if you feel that way most of the time? Is that when you put on your khakis and put a note in your back pocket?

And then go floating off a concrete bridge and then off the planet?

I've been walking a long, long time. The butterflies must've come and gone in the little dude's backyard.

The other day we got a shipment of butterfly nets. I opened them up and almost snatched one of them up and ran to the cash register to buy it, because butterfly net! Little dude!

八十九

But here's the thing: the little dude isn't a hunter of butterflies. He's an admirer of butterflies. So I fill a big basket with the nets and then I make a sign.

INVISIBLE GHOST CATCHERS! TO BE USED
ONLY FOR CATCHING INVISIBLE GHOSTS!

Because imagine all the little kids out there with invisible ghosts waking them up at night, freaked out, and if they have an invisible ghost catcher, they'll be ready.

I wasn't ready for my dad to die. Who is, right? Who's ready for a lot of the shit that goes down in a life?

No one, maybe.

It's late. Late on a Tuesday night and there's a
bag of blessings in my hand and a bag of cornmeal
under the Bowie T-shirt that I still can't let go of.

And a note on the table: *Free Willy! Love, Mom.*

I draw a fang-face smiley under it. She likes them.

Whatever.

More salt this time, some dried chili peppers, a can
of corn, drained. Whatever. Does the butter hiss? The
butter hisses. But does it taste good?

Nope. Not even with a ton of butter. Whatever the
secret recipe is, I don't know it.

Whatever, whatever, whatever, whatever.

By the time I'm done with the latest cornbread failure and the hiding of failure evidence, it's like three a.m. and all of L.A.'s asleep. Maybe.

I pack up Playa's gift of the day. An invisible ghost catcher. Because invisible ghost catchers aren't just for little kids. You know? I shove the failed cornbread into my backpack next to the gift bag and head out. It's dark as hell. Later than late.

Wait, did I remember her note? No.

Don't let the bastards get you down.

You don't need to see in order to write a note. That one, anyway.

I'm walking past the weed lot, the one they keep trying to turn into a community garden, when I hear what at first, thanks to Major Tom, I think is my name:

"Dolla?"

But it's not. It's Superman.

"Late for you, isn't it, Superman?"

"Dolla?"

Whatever happened to Superman happened long ago, because as long as I can remember, he has been sitting against the wall, any wall on First.

"You hungry, Superman?"

He nods. Holds out his hand. Here you go, friend. A dollar and some failed cornbread for you. *Carry on, my wayward son.*

I keep on walking.

九十三

Past Taco Loco, past Estella's Panaderia, past closed-up PAWN PAWN PAWN. Past an apartment building with someone practicing guitar in a third-floor window.

Music, the refuge of the lonely.

Playa walks the halls at school, friends watching over her. *She's going to need to be tough,* my mom said.

Her house is dark. Her steps are dark. The white bag is a white shadow in the darkness. I stand on the top step and spread my arms. I'm taking a stand for Superman. For the little dude. For Major Tom. For my mom and her notes. For—

"Will?"

Oh shit.

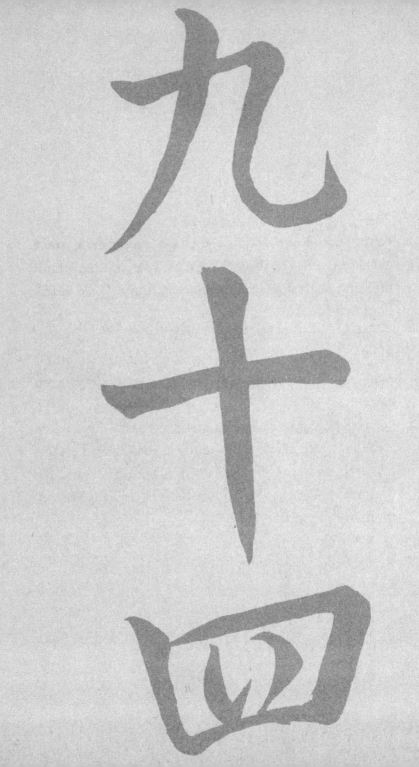

She eases the door open and slips through it. She's like a ghost. White T-shirt, white shorts. Dark hair that you can't see in the dark.

Invisible ghost catchers! To be used only for catching invisible ghosts!

"I knew it was you," she says.

It's too dark to see her face. Which means it's too dark for her to see my face, right? She reaches down and picks up the little white ghost bag, sways it back and forth from her invisible finger.

"Ghost man," she says. "Sneaking around leaving presents for people."

Ghost man. Is she a mind reader?

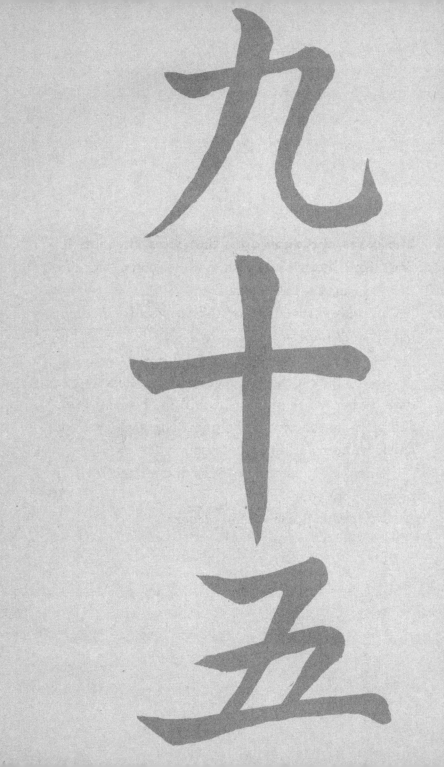

What do I say? Playa is a ghost girl and I'm a ghost boy and the little white gift bag is a ghost gift and we're sitting on the top step in the dark, ghosts all around us.

"Playa," I say.

She doesn't say anything. Just swings the little bag from her invisible hand. I try again.

"Playa."

But nothing comes out after that, because shit, I'm crying. I try to keep it silent so she doesn't know, but she knows. I can tell by the way her invisible hand comes out and touches my shoulder.

"It's okay," she says.

九十六

It's not okay. It is NOT okay. Jesus. We both know that. Her hand disappears and then comes back with something in it.

"Here," she says. I wipe my face with it, this soft and familiar thing. Smells like powder.

"Is this—?"

"Yeah. It's my blankie."

Playa the ring champion, Playa the ghost girl. Playa the tough.

It's awful, having to be tough.

But I don't talk about that. I talk about the cornbread, how I keep trying to re-create it when my mom's working the overnight, but how no matter what I try, it's a fail. That it sucks.

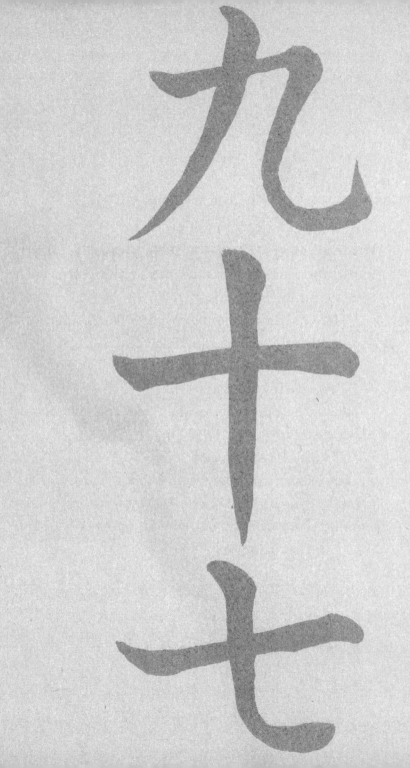

"His cornbread sucked too, though," she says. "Remember?"

"Wait, what?"

"Will, your dad was great. But his cornbread? Nasty."

There in the dark she shakes her head. Playa, who has to be tough. Playa, who knew my dad. It comes to me then, comes washing over me, that she's right.

My dad's cornbread sucked.

"But everyone loved my dad," I say. "Didn't they?"

"Yeah," she says. "They did. Same as everyone loves you. I guess love isn't cornbread-dependent."

She laughs. A tiny laugh. First time I've heard Playa laugh since it happened.

Time to leave the capsule if you dare.

九十八

Somewhere out there I hope Major Tom's asleep, and Dear Mrs. Lin, and the little butterfly dude.

Superman's not asleep. He's awake and against a wall, maybe eating cornbread and maybe thinking it's not that shitty.

And not my mom. She's not asleep. My mom is at the hospital, working the overnight. Maybe she's sitting by someone's bed. Maybe she's at the nurse's station, eating her dinner. Which I don't even know what it is, come to think of it.

Maybe she's composing a note in her head. A note to her son, making sure he knows she loves him.

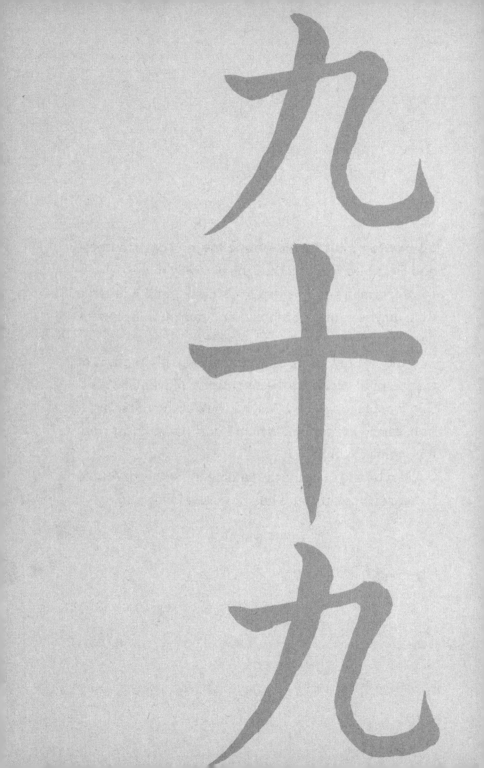

A long time ago, a father used to wear a Bowie T-shirt. He used to make cornbread. He used to tell his kid secrets, like melt the butter, like only use cast iron. He used to sing Bowie songs while he worked. He sang about Major Tom and ground control, about sitting in a tin can far above the world, how Planet Earth was blue and there was nothing he could do. He used to tell his kid that music was the refuge of the lonely, and to carry on, that blessings are everywhere you look, even in the dark.

Me and Playa, we've left the capsule and we're walking down the street, looking up, the way artists do. Stars here and there, even in smoggy L.A.

"Will," she says. "You got through what happened with your dad, right? And I'll get through this, right?"

Correction: I'm *getting* through what happened with my dad. That's not what I say, though.

"Yes," is what I say.

"Don't let the bastards get you down," she says. "Right?"

I'm nodding. A ghost girl and a ghost boy walking through the dark, earth below and stars above, not letting the bastards get us down.

Acknowledgments

This book holds within its pages much of my heart. Life is beautiful and it is hard. Like others, I have lived through the bewildering grief of suicide, anguished over others' pain due to sexual assault, and walked my way through times that felt unbearable. Will's dad told him that blessings are everywhere you look, even in the dark, and I believe that. I thank the people in my life who have made a cloud of safety around me, especially Mark Garry; my mother and father; my sisters; my children; my friends Ellen Harris Swiggett and Julie Schumacher; and my beloved brother, Doug. Thanks to Sherman Ng for the beautiful calligraphy. Love to my agents, Sara and Heather, both of whom were integral to this book. More love, and eternal gratitude, to Caitlyn Dlouhy, who still and always coaxes my books to their best selves.

My deep thanks to all my Chinese language students at South High School. You were my crucible for so much. It was in that windowless classroom that I first learned how to teach and how to listen to the stories you told me. Stories hurt, stories heal, stories save our lives. I look back on those years with love and gratitude. *Wo ai nimen.*

To those readers struggling with feelings of hopelessness and despair, please know that you are not alone. There are people who will help you. Here are two good resources:

1. If you are dealing with depression or if you are thinking of suicide, call 1-800-273-TALK (8255) or text NAMI to 741-741 for help.

2. If you have been sexually assaulted by someone, call 1-800-656-4673 or text RAINN for help.

A Reading Group Guide to

WHAT I LEAVE BEHIND

By Alison McGhee

About the Book

"Sometimes you got to walk the day out of you."
That's what sixteen-year-old Will does. He walks.
And as he walks, he thinks about the homeless
man on the street, the lonely little boy who loves
butterflies, or the dog who lives his life on a chain.
Full of empathy, Will discovers that acts of kindness
not only help others, but they begin to help him
come to terms with his father's suicide. Told in
beautifully crafted chapters of one hundred words
each and over one hundred pages, *What I Leave
Behind* shows how the universe can reveal itself in
mysterious ways, and how, with an open heart, the
most broken hearts can be healed.

Questions for Group Discussion

1. Will is highly sensitive and observant. Early
in the story, he thinks, *Tonight the air itself is
dark. That happens sometimes. It's not just the*

lack of sun, it's the presence of darkness. What do you think Will means by this thought?

2. Will has an understanding of human nature that goes well beyond his sixteen years. Discuss the character traits that make Will a sympathetic character. How are Will's social skills an asset to him?

3. "Music is the refuge of the lonely" is an adage that Will's father often said. What is a refuge? Do you agree with this adage? Explain. Offer examples from personal experience.

4. People who are awkward around others are often unfairly labeled as odd or weird. Will realizes this about Major Tom early in their relationship. How does Will interact with Major Tom? What does he understand about Major Tom's nature? Will compares his own social skills to a "dance where you're born knowing the steps." Discuss what he means by this description. How can you use Will as a model for interacting with new people?

5. Small moments, gestures, and phrases can flood Will with emotion: Major Tom closing his eyes

and jabbing his finger on one of his motivational quotes, little butterfly dude putting the binoculars up to his eyes, or everyone on the bus laughing at the Cheese Doodles–eating kid. What do these reactions tell you about Will? Why do such seemingly simple and arbitrary moments move him?

6. What is a mantra? How is Will's walking like a mantra? How does the physical activity of walking help Will move through the grieving process? In addition to the physical activity, what thoughts and experiences does Will have along the way that help him begin to come to terms with his loss? How does helping others in pain help him deal with his own pain?

7. Readers learn that Playa was gang-raped at a party. Enraged, Will's mom says, "I don't care if Angie got drunk. I don't care if Playa fell asleep.... You're telling me that's why they locked the door and raped her? Like that's the only logical outcome? That's the *explanation*?" Discuss Will's mom's statement and the questions she poses, and how it relates to conversations surrounding rape culture today. Focus on the word explanation.

8. Will references a former art teacher who used to say, "Look around, artists. The world is full of mystery." How is this line representative of Will's interactions with the world? Do you think mystery is one of the themes of *What I Leave Behind*? If so, cite examples from the text to support your opinion. If not, explain why.

9. Why is Will drawn to little butterfly dude? Why does the image of the boy sitting with folded hands come to Will after he gives the jump rope to the little girl in aisle seven? What is the significance of little butterfly dude's altar? Why does it affect Will so deeply?

10. How does Will connect Playa's rape to the last word he said to his father? Why do you think Will wonders if he should have seen warning signs before Playa's rape and his father's suicide? Do you think it's common to look back on a loss and think you could or should have done something to prevent it?

11. The main source of Will's anger and remorse is finally revealed in a confession to Playa about his father: "*Nah.* That was the last thing I said to

my dad. I refused his cornbread. Don't tell me it's not important, don't tell me that's a stupid thing to care about, don't tell me my dad would understand, don't tell me to give up on the fucking recipe. You are not the one who stood there late to school on the last day you would see your dad and said *NAH*." For Will, what would "giving up on the recipe" signify? In addition to anger, what other emotions do you think he's feeling?

12. Discuss Will's plan to give Playa one hundred gifts. Is Playa the only one benefitting from this plan? Why is it so important for him to give her these gifts? Why do you think Will finally breaks down with Playa?

13. Why is the shift in Major Tom's tone when he tells Will to go home an important moment in the story? Why do you think Will tells Major Tom that he's going to make cornbread? What does this moment reveal about Major Tom? What does it reveal about Will's journey toward healing?

14. Will's father died of suicide. Discuss the following passage: "It's different, suicide. It's a different kind of death. Most people, they'll do

anything to stay alive, right? Past the point where you're looking at them and thinking, *Wow. Your life must* suck. *Don't you, like want to die*? But most people don't. They just want to keep on living." Do you agree with Will? Is suicide "different"? Why is Will glad "in a way" that his father left a suicide note?

15. Will wonders whether his father feels "like he was one thing on the outside and something else entirely different on the inside." What does this statement mean to you? Do you think all people feel this way? How might this be an aspect of being human?

16. Discuss the passages in which Will relates the story about Playa on the playground rings. How does this story illustrate their personal connection, and why is this a scene for Will that "just burns and burns its way into you"?

17. "Carry On Wayward Son" is the title of a 1970s song by the rock band Kansas. The chorus lyrics are as follows: "Carry on my wayward son/There'll be peace when you are done/Lay your weary head to rest/Don't you cry no more." How does Will

carry on with his life after his dad's suicide? How do the lyrics reflect actions and characters in the story?

18. Why do you think Will decides to go to the blessings store? What is he trying to find there? Mrs. Lin calls Will a good friend. How do his actions prove that he is a good friend? What does it mean to "have someone's back"?

19. Along Will's walking path, he encounters people and animals that cause him to think deeply about life: little butterfly dude, Superman, the dog of Insanity, Major Tom, Playa. What do these characters have in common? Why do you think Will feels compelled to help them all?

20. Discuss Will's notion of an "early warning system" as protection from things that "claw at your heart." Why does Will relate so deeply with the dog of Insanity?

21. Discuss Will's relationship with Major Tom. How does it change over the course of the story? How did it surprise you or make you think differently about people and how you treat them?

22. Why does Will keep trying to re-create the cornbread that his father used to make? Why does he hide the cast iron skillet and cornmeal in his room? Why do you think his attempts always fail? What does the cornbread symbolize? How does Playa telling Will that his father's cornbread "sucked" become a catalyst that helps him to express his grief? What does she mean when she says, "I guess love isn't cornbread-dependent"?

23. Grief and loss are two of the main themes in *What I Leave Behind*. Discuss how Will processes his emotions throughout the story. Discuss the significance of ghosts, including Will's references to a cornbread ghost and invisible ghost catchers. Why does Will refer to Playa and himself as "a ghost girl and a ghost boy"?

24. Consider the title, *What I Leave Behind*. How does this relate to Will's actions in the story? How is memory something that is left behind?

Activities
"Ground Control to Major Tom"
Lyrics from "Space Oddity," a song by the late singer-songwriter David Bowie, appear throughout

the story. Read the "Space Oddity" lyrics and listen to the song. Discuss what is happening in the song on a literal level and how many of the lines connect to the story. How does the theme of "Space Oddity" relate to the characters and events in *What I Leave Behind*?

The Blessings Store

Readers learn about the blessings store early in the text, but Will doesn't visit until much later. Three blessings in particular speak to Will, and read like poetry: "To unbreak your broken heart/ To make a cloud of safety around you/To light at night for peace." Think about blessings that you would bestow upon someone special in your life. Following the above lines as a model, write a series of ten blessings that are meaningful to you.

One Hundred Pages, One Hundred Words

Author Alison McGhee constructed *What I Leave Behind* in a unique way: each of the one hundred pages of text contains exactly one hundred words. Discuss how this structure defies the traditional way of writing chapters and how it relates to poetry. Then write a short story that follows the same format, allowing only one hundred words per page.

Random Acts of Kindness

Throughout the story, Will helps people in need. Although he is grieving over his father, he still manages to care about others. Brainstorm some local causes or organizations in your area and plan how you can come to the aid of these people in need, whether you donate time, gifts, or other means of support. Consider activities such as making cards for sick children or collecting spare change to donate to a charity.

Backstories

Will notices Major Tom's snaggle tooth when he "smiles for real." This moment leads Will to the following thought: "A story makes itself up in my head, him as a little kid and his mom making him grilled cheese and teasing him about his snaggle tooth, but in a nice-mom kind of way." Write backstories for one or more of the following characters in the form of three to five vignettes, each depicting a possible memory of their pasts: Major Tom, little butterfly dude, Superman, Mrs. Lin, or Playa. Share your pieces with the class.

This guide has been provided by Simon & Schuster for classroom, library, and reading group use. It may be reproduced in its entirety or excerpted for these purposes.

RIVETED

BY *simon* teen ♥

BELIEVE IN YOUR SHELF

Visit RivetedLit.com & connect with us on social to:

DISCOVER NEW YA READS

READ BOOKS FOR FREE

DISCUSS YOUR FAVORITES

SHARE YOUR IDEAS

ENTER SWEEPSTAKES FOR THE CHANCE TO WIN BOOKS

Follow @SimonTeen on

to stay up to date with all things Riveted!

Check out these gripping stories from *New York Times* bestselling author

JASON REYNOLDS

"An unexpectedly gorgeous meditation on the meaning of family, the power of friendship, and the value of loyalty."

—*Booklist*
on *When I Was the Greatest*

"A vivid, satisfying, and ultimately upbeat tale of grief, redemption, and grace."

—*Kirkus Reviews*
on *The Boy in the Black Suit*

★"Timely and powerful, this novel promises to have an impact long after the pages stop turning."

—*School Library Journal*,
on *All American Boys*,
starred review

Skint's in the Pit because of Dinah. So she figures she better get cracking and affect his speedy release. Dinah would go to the **ends of the earth and back** if it would help Skint.

But is it possible to try too hard to save your best friend?

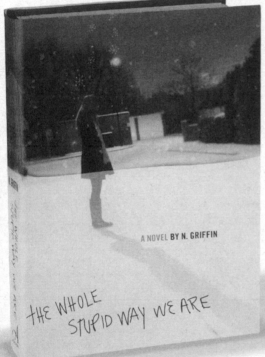

"So furious, so heartbreaking. . . . A thing of beauty, that's what this is."
—Kathi Appelt, author of
The Underneath, a Newbery Honor book